BIG**FAT**

Voyeur

Hedonist

Hedonist

CONTENTS

BIG FAT VOYEUR

Him:

Every day I watch her. Every day a little more of me dies.

My modest flat up on the fifteenth floor used to be my sanctuary. My quiet corner of the world where nobody would bother me and I could just *be*. But now, it has been infiltrated by a sickness I cannot control.

Just another glimpse. Just one more image of her, captured in secret on my phone to refer to later when I'm in bed. And even when I'm not.

The girl in the flat opposite me, in various states of undress. From the moment she arrives home from work every day, my sweet torture begins. She likes to kick back on the sofa, dressed only in lingerie, while she enjoys her nightly glass of red wine. Sometimes she prepares her dinner in just a shirt with nothing underneath… And sometimes she leaves the bedroom curtains open just enough for me to catch a glimpse of her on the covers as she goes about her grooming routines.

Why doesn't she just close the fucking curtains already? Why unknowingly invite me, an unwanted and depraved spectator into her life? Camera in one hand, cock in the other. Because there's no way she'd do it on purpose. There's no way she'd look at me, all four-hundred-and-who-knows-how-many pounds of me and thought, '*Hmm… Now there's a guy I want lusting after me every night!*'

I've seen the way she looked at me when she passed me in the street some days ago. The subtlest hint of a smile playing on her lips. As if I wouldn't realise she was laughing at me. Ridiculing me in her thoughts. The fucking whore.

The worst part is the guilt.

Because as much as I hate her, I'm starting to love her too. That, in turn, makes me hate myself even more. Like, what the fuck am I even doing? I'm losing what's left of my humanity, every single time I rub one out while spying on her.

It's not that my life was that great before she moved in. Far from it.

But it's easier to ignore just how lonely you are when you don't come face-to-face with everything you wish you had. Every night. Inside the flat opposite mine. Outside my window and inside hers.

Whoever thought designing a block of flats with a U-shaped floor plan like this was a good idea needs to burn in hell. At least stagger the fucking windows so you don't look right into someone's private space! Barely thirty feet away…

I'm bracing myself for the inevitable night when it won't just be her in there. Because girls like that rarely stay single long. Will she still keep the curtains open? Will I carry on watching? That'll be a true test of my newfound misery.

Her:

Every day I see him. The guy in the flat opposite me. Far away and yet so very close.

I know he's watching; I can feel his eyes on me like a hot breeze caressing my naked skin. And the more he watches, the further I want to take things. It's a little game I like to play.

I have to picture what he might look like when he does it, since he keeps his lights dimmed most of the time. His big fat body must be covered in sweat as he jerks himself off to the sight of me in various states of undress. I wish I could see the look in his eyes up close. The strain in his expression when he's getting to the point of no return. The inevitable groans and moans that escape his lips when he deposits a sticky load into his fist.

Again and again and again, for eight nights in a row now. I don't know how many times a night.

I wonder if he's sore yet. Because I am.

I'm aching just thinking about how he must feel; or at least how I hope he feels. Because that's how I feel too… Despair doesn't quite describe it. Misery is more like it.

We don't know each other. I tried smiling at him once or twice in the street. I doubt he even noticed. He was too busy on his phone to even care. But as soon as I realised he lived right across from me, I put my plan into action. Once I got home from work, I kicked off my shoes, jeans, t-shirt and more… All with the curtains and windows wide open. Barely a stone's throw away from where he was sitting around, watching TV. Before he switched off his lights, I saw him. Eyes locked onto my position.

His curtains never closed either after that. That's how I knew I had earned his undivided attention. The only indication that he was even home has been the flicker of the TV in the background.

And so I've been doing this every night since. Get home, slip into something more comfortable, and act like a fucking cock tease just to get a rise out of him.

It's our little secret.

I leave the curtains open. He enjoys the view inside mine.

But for how long can we keep this up? How long until I die of impatience and give the game away?

Right now, both of us can feign ignorance. We can pretend like I'm not doing it on purpose, and he's not really looking. But once I confront him about it, that's when suddenly everything will change. Am I ready for it? Is he?

There's only one way to find out.

Him:

I log onto one of the many forums for guys just like me, on the dark corners of the web, just to bemoan my predicament. Just to vent.

"I have a new neighbour in the flat right across from me in my apartment complex. My windows overlook hers perfectly. She's a

hot little thing. Blonde. Legs for miles. Tight little ass and a perfect pair of tits…"

I sigh and pinch the bridge of my nose. Would it have mattered if she wasn't a ten out of ten? Probably not. I'd still be looking. I'd still be aching for her. And she'd still be infinitely out of reach. But I leave the description in there, just to paint a picture of the extent of my problem.

"Every evening she comes home from work, strips down to her underwear and parades around her flat with the curtains wide open. I can't look away. I can't think. I can't do a damn thing, except stare at her and drink. God, I've been drinking so much to try and numb myself. And jerk off to the sight of her, of course."

As shameful as my confession is, it's still a relief just to get it out there. It's not like I have anyone else to talk to as it is.

"I'm sore. I'm exhausted. I'm miserable. I can't think of anything else all day except how I want to tear that ass up and pound the shit out of her. Every single day. This has been going on for nearly two weeks now."

My fingers are tingling. I ball my fist, then stretch out a few times in quick succession just to make it stop. It doesn't.

"If she knew what I was doing, she'd call the cops on me and it'd be justified. The few times I've passed her in the street I could tell she was laughing at me. Mostly that's what women do, anyway. Laugh. Stare. Point. I guess at around four-fifty and change, I'm an easy enough target. Nobody sees me as a man. Nobody realises I have urges too."

I open another can of beer and down about half of it

in one go. I'm going to have to try something harder to take the edge off at this rate.

"Anyway, brothers. What the fuck do I do? I can't relocate; my flat is rent controlled and I don't have the $$$ for anything else. I don't have the self-discipline to look away. I'm going crazy over here! This bitch will take my last shred of sanity."

Submit.

I blankly stare out the window, where her flat is as yet empty and dark. Then I down the rest of my beer and crush the can in my hand before throwing it to the floor. One more for the collection of trash that's already lying all around me.

Responses to my post start to come in pretty quickly. None are particularly helpful.

"Pictures, or it didn't happen."

I roll my eyes, but then… I do have hundreds of pictures. Maybe a thousand already. I could find one that wasn't too revealing. One that doesn't show her face, only the rest of her.

Before I get the chance to act on that dumbass idea, another reply comes in.

"Stop beating yourself up, man. If she's got the curtains open, you're justified to look. She's a fucking tease and she knows it."

Okay… but that doesn't help me deal with this, does it?

"Go over there and give her the good pounding she deserves! Fucking whore."

I shake my head. Easy for you to say, keyboard warrior!

Yet another one comes in.

"This is exactly what I've been talking about! These bitches act like they own the whole fucking world, and meanwhile it's good guys like the OP whose lives are being made miserable. Everything is skewed against us nowadays. Bitches should wear what they want, but we're not allowed to touch or even look. They can push us to the brink, but then say 'no', laugh and get away with it, because apparently that's what 'consent' looks like. Fuck that. Why don't you call the cops on her instead? Tell them she's been exposing herself while your neighbour's kids were watching."

I lean back against the sofa and sigh deeply while shaking my head. I can't do that to her, can I? This isn't her problem, it's mine. She's just out there, living her life…

I'm the pervert who's making a big deal out of this. Why can't I just enjoy it? Why does it always have to be all or nothing with me? I can't have her, so she should get in trouble with the law? What sort of logic is that?

A notification pops up on my screen. The same guy who first commented on my thread has sent me a private message now.

*"Srsly. You *do* have pics, right?"*

I throw away the phone in disgust.

Her:

The flash coming from his window attracts my attention. I wouldn't have noticed, if I hadn't already been looking there because it's still light out. But now that I know, I can't ignore it.

My heart is racing.

He's taking pictures of me.

What does he do with them?

Does he keep them for himself or is he uploading them for others to see? If it's the former, it's exciting. The latter... A delicious shiver runs up and down my spine and intensifies the ache in my cunt.

I get up from the bed and stand right by the window. Eyes fixed on the darkness that lies beyond the open curtains of his flat, and both hands flat against the glass.

Take a picture of me again! Come on, I dare you!

There's some movement at his place. A shadow passing by the flickering light of the television as he changes his position. Is he trying to get a better angle?

I wait for another flash. Another indication that the game is still on.

I keep standing there, in my teeny-tiny little lace bra and panty set, in full view just so he can get a good shot of me.

And then... I wait.

Nothing.

A shiver passes down my spine. Suddenly I'm vulnerable and alone.

Because I don't feel him anymore. His eyes are no longer on me. I'm no longer being watched. Where the fuck did he go? Why would he have left halfway through the epic show I had planned out for him?

Is it because of that flash? Because I saw it, and came up to the window, and thus he could no longer pretend that what he was doing was his little secret? Is he embarrassed? There's no need to be.

The image on the TV changes over to something else. Its light brightens the room. Normally when this happens, I'd be able to see his silhouette on the couch. Not anymore.

I keep looking, with my breath held, willing him to come back.

He doesn't. Minutes pass and his flat remains empty.

Instead, I pick up some movement with the corner of my eye. The outline of a person, where I've never seen anyone before. Where no one should ever be, under normal circumstances. Fuck!

There's someone on the roof, a couple of stories up from where both our flats are.

I squint and stare at the figure up top and feel all hope drain from my heart. It has to be him. Who else? He's a big man; unmistakably big. It's so obvious now that it's him. And he's approaching the edge of the building, slowly, steadily. It's that same signature walk I've come to know so well.

Goddammit, this can't be good! I force myself into action and open the balcony door, before stepping out into the fresh breeze.

"No!" I call out, and wave both my arms. "No! Stop!"

I don't even know his name. Fuck. Even if I did, I don't think he would be able to hear me. Or he's ignoring me. Either way, it's absolutely pointless what I'm doing.

I scan the other flats opposite me. Nobody else is out there. Not a single soul who could call for help. My phone is inside somewhere, and anyway, there's no fucking time. Even if I call someone, they'd take at least half an hour to get here.

Instead of dawdling any more, I make a run for it. To the door, out the hallway, straight to the elevators.

I've never been more grateful to live in this weird U-shaped building than right now. If I ride the elevator all the way to the top floor, run along the hallway to his wing and find the stairs leading up to the roof, I should end up exactly where he is.

As soon as the doors open, I rush inside and start stabbing the button for the eighteenth floor until finally, the doors close again. The ascent is slow and torturous. What the fuck is he playing at! I'm not going to be too late, am I?

Finally, the elevator arrives on the correct floor and I again make a run for it. My bare feet make a distinctive slapping noise as they hit the tiled hallway. *Pat, pat, pat, pat.* Straight ahead and around the corner at the end, until I reach his wing of the apartment complex.

I can't breathe. I can't think. I just have to get there in time.

It's an absolute miracle I don't bump into anyone. A miracle, or a disaster, because maybe then I could get them to call the police or someone. Who do you even call for something like this? The fire department, maybe?

But help isn't coming. I am the help, or trying to be.

Once I make it across, I find myself in a hallway that looks identical to all the others in this building, except on the top floor, there's an emergency staircase that goes up. . I race towards it and start climbing. If he's up there, the door is bound to be unlocked still.

I hope.

I climb the remaining two flights of stairs until I make it to the top. And sure enough, the door to the roof, covered in warning stickers and 'no trespassing' signs is indeed ajar.

I push against it until I can make it through, completely out of breath and stumbling over my own feet in the process.

"Wait! Don't do it!"

The wind is quite a bit stronger up here than it was on my own balcony. It's rather loud and drowns out most of my voice as well. But I see him. He's still there, standing at the far edge of the roof, looking down with his back towards me.

I start running again, ignoring how the rough tarred surface of the roof bites into the soles of my feet. And how my chest is trying to strangle my lungs with every breath. Trying not to trip over any stray hoses and pipes littering the distance that still remains between him and me. The cold air prickles against my skin as every single hair on my arms and legs stands up to attention.

"Wait! Stop!" I call out, pausing a few feet away from him and panting desperately for air.

He turns and looks at me. His eyes are watery, unfocused. Has he been crying? His formerly impressive physique actually looks so much smaller now than every single time I've passed him in the street. Deflated.

Defeated. He looks broken, and that in turn breaks me too. What the fuck happened?

"Don't!" I plead, raising both arms up in a defensive gesture.

"Why not?" he asks. His baritone voice is flat. It occurs to me that we've never even had a conversation before now. Except in my imagination.

"Because…"

He scoffs. "You don't have an answer."

"Well, do *you*?" I counter. "Do you have an answer for why you want to do this?"

"Yeah, about a million!" he sounds hurt. Like a cornered animal. It tears at my heartstrings.

"Tell me,"

"Because I'm a stain on this world. A mistake. I shouldn't be here."

"What? Why do you say that?"

"Really? You still have to ask? After everything I've done to you?"

I shake my head. "We don't even know each other yet. How can you have done anything to me?"

He closes his eyes and fresh tears roll down his cheeks. Getting stuck momentarily in his rather impressive beard before dripping down onto his broad shoulders where they leave dark stains on the cotton of his t-shirt.

"You saw the flash. Don't deny it."

"Yeah, so?" I ask.

"I've been watching you. I'm so sorry." He shakes his head.

"At least come closer while you talk to me. I can hardly hear you over the wind," I plead.

"I can't." He shakes his head again, faster.

"Yes you can." I hold out my hand in his direction. It's shaking. I'm shaking all over. "Please. I would feel a lot better if you stepped away from the edge."

"No! I have to do this. It'll be the only good decision I've ever made in my life."

"Why, because you've been watching me every single night? Taking pictures?" I ask.

He nods. "Yeah, that and…"

I take a deep breath and try to focus. And… And, what? I have to tell him somehow that it's okay. That I don't mind. He has nothing to feel guilty about.

"Ever wonder why I keep my curtains open?" I ask.

He frowns and looks up at me. "It was a trap. You were waiting for me to slip up, and now I have. You've probably already called the police."

"I did. I did call the police. Because I saw you up here and was afraid of what you were going to do," I lie.

"See! So I really don't have any other way out." "No, stop!" I call out. "Please, don't do this."

He turns away from me and shakes his head. "You really shouldn't be here. I can't-- Not with *you* here."

"I'm not fucking leaving."

He turns again and glares at me. "I can't even look at you! You're disgusting!"

My heart is pounding in my throat, but I resist the urge to look away and keep staring back at him. Even if his words are hurtful. Even if I'm so raw now, I'm about to cry too. "You want me to go? Make me! Drag me to the stairs by my hair and barricade the door behind me. Come on, do it, big man! If you've got the balls, then do it right now!" I scream.

He inhales sharply and closes his eyes. "I can't, I can't, I can't," his voice is monotone, almost like he's reciting a mantra or prayer.

"You can't, what? You can't come over here and get rid of me? You can only look from afar like a fucking pussy?" I taunt him. I should feel bad about this, but maybe the end justifies the means.

"Fuck," he spits. "You've been making my life hell for weeks. And now you're making my last minutes hell too. This is exactly the problem with you... You..."

His words shock me. Just how in the actual fuck have I been--

"You bitches!" he finally says. It maybe was meant to come out as a curse, but it sounds more like a question. Like he's confused with what he's trying to say.

"All I wanted was your attention," I say. Jesus, I feel terrible. Guilty. Crushed. I wanted to have a bit of fun with him. And now... Have my games inadvertently hurt him? Is this all my fault?

He looks at me again and his shoulders slump even further. "You, wanted *what?*"

"Your attention. It's why I kept my curtains open. Just for you." My throat feels so tight, it might just close up entirely. And my heart is still racing out of control, making me feel faint. And the first tears start to break free too.

"You've been taunting me. You've been--"

I shake my head and sniffle.

"Every time we passed each other in the street, I could see you laughing at me. You were kind of trying to suppress it, but..."

"Goddammit, I was *smiling at you!*" I throw my hands up in despair. Did he really just misinterpret every single fucking attempt I made at flirting with him? Seriously?! Do I suck that badly?

"Smiling? Why would you be smiling at me?" he says, as if he's talking to himself and not me. I can't even be angry at him anymore. I'm more angry at myself.

"Come here and find out!" I hook my finger in his direction.

He stumbles a few steps in my direction, until the gap between us closes just enough for me to make my move. I charge ahead and fling my arms around his shoulders, clinging on for dear life.

"You still wanna jump, you're taking me with you," I sob.

"Have you lost your fucking mind?"

The adrenaline is starting to wear off, leaving me a shivering, blubbering mess. I'm feeling cold as well, more so because of how warm he is. So very warm.

But I don't let go. I tighten my arms around his neck and press my face up against the side of his. He's so tense. So tightly wound. But the longer I stand there, leaning against him and crying into his shoulder, the more he begins to melt under my touch.

"This would have been a dream, if only…" he sighs. "If only it wasn't such a nightmare as well."

"What do you mean?" I lean back to look up at him through clumpy wet lashes.

"You do realise you're not wearing any clothes, right?" he stares at my lips for a moment, then down at my cleavage, spilling out of the tiny little bra I'd put on especially to tease him with tonight.

"Oh." The realisation makes me smile just a little. "I guess, I *really* needed to get your attention. More than ever."

He winces and looks away from me. "You don't play fair."

"So. You were saying something about this being like a dream… Does that mean my nightly performances were having the desired effect? At least a little?"

He makes a face and looks away. "Look, I don't know what your game is. But I'm not a player. I don't know--"

"It's very simple."

He glances into my eyes for a moment. God, he looks so miserable. Just why, I have no idea. But I have to try and make it better or I'll never be able to live with myself. There's just something about him that makes me want to throw caution in the wind and just go for it. Now or never.

"I first noticed you two days after I moved in. While I was coming back from the corner shop. I wanted to say 'hi', but you looked so fucking stern, I chickened out," I explain.

His eyebrows crunch up together. "I thought you were just staring. Everyone stares."

"Maybe I was. But only because I was trying to build up the nerve to talk to you."

"Why would you want that?"

"Because I liked what I saw. You're cute."

His frown deepens. "Now I know you're just shitting me."

I shake my head. "I would never."

Shit, even now, his eyes are dreamy, his beard is gloriously thick and his larger-than-life body. Holy hell, the things I would do to him, if given half a chance.

"You're playing me. Keeping me talking long enough until the cops get here and you'll have me arrested for stalking you."

"I'm pretty sure I provoked that. They'd have to take me away in cuffs too. Plus, I'm out here exposing myself in public, as you've already reminded me of. That's probably a crime too."

He stares at me again.

"This would have been a dream for me too," I whisper, while caressing the rough hair on his cheek, with the back of my fingers. "Under different circumstances."

He swallows hard and closes his eyes. His chest rises and falls in short bursts beneath my embrace. I think I've got him. I've finally got him.

"Wanna hear a secret?" I whisper in his ear. "Just as I didn't get the chance to put on clothes, before rushing over here. I never got the chance to call the police either."

"You never…" His voice trembles. "Fuck. Please stop toying with me."

He tries to take a step back, but I don't let go. He's so strong, he ends up dragging me across the floor.

"This sort of thing doesn't just happen. This *can't* happen."

"Why not?" I ask. "You don't want me touching you?" I run my hand through his hair and enjoy how my chest begins to flutter and my cunt starts to tingle with excitement. "You don't like having my half-naked woman pressed up into you like this?"

He's so damn tense, I'm worried he might pop a vein. "I… Fucking hell! This isn't supposed to happen to me."

"But, it is happening."

"I have nobody, okay? Never had. I'm a failure of a human being. Lazy, selfish, pathetic. A loser. A fat, ugly loser, who is destined to die alone."

He's crying again. It breaks my heart.

"Baby. Why?"

"Nobody has ever given a toss about me. Nobody will miss me when I'm gone."

"I would! I would miss you. I've been looking forward to our little game the whole day, every day," I whisper.

"Not if you really knew me. Not if you knew how I've been sitting on my ass the whole day, drinking, stuffing junk food into my face, jerking off to photos I took of you in secret the night before. How I've rubbed myself so raw, I'm actually hurting. I have literally done nothing except stroke myself all day. Every day. Every night."

"Well, what do you think I've been doing? With the curtains wide open so you could see…"

"I could think of nothing except tearing up your tight little pussy and filling you up with my cum. Up to ten times a day. Every. Single. Day."

I inhale sharply and grab his face. "Baby, don't you tease me now."

Is he serious? Ten times a day? Have I finally found a guy so virile he could keep up with me?

His eyes snap open again and he stares me down. It gives me butterflies.

"You're playing with fire, little girl." His voice is deeper now. Rougher.

Rawr!

"I like it hot."

I reach downward, running my hand across his big, fat body, fondling and squeezing my way across his chest, his sides, his huge sagging belly, until… I cup my fingers across his crotch.

He flinches and his face turns red and sweaty.

"Does it hurt?" I ask, sweetly.

He nods. "So much."

"It'll feel much better once it's inside of me."

He swallows blankly and fails to steady his breath.

I rub my hand across the very obvious bulge in his sweatpants, causing him to shudder and nuzzle the side of my neck.

Everything he's told me so far has only made me hotter. And I've finally figured out that the best way to distract him from what he's about to do just happens to be the thing I've perfected for two whole weeks. I'm being such a slut. Just for him.

"Baby. What do you say we go downstairs."

He tenses again. "No! You're just fucking with me!"

I shake my head. "Not yet. But I will."

"I can't do this. I can't--"

Oh god. Every time he protests, I want to double down. It's a challenge now. I must have him. In my bed. Between my thighs. I won't accept no for an answer.

"I want you. I want you to show me how many times you can cum tonight, so long as it's inside of me! We won't let a single drop go to waste," I demand.

He whimpers and grinds his hips in my direction. Hell yeah, he wants it. He can't help himself!

"I want to feel you unload into me. Again and again and again!" I urge.

"Oh fuck," he groans.

"I'd do it right here, right now, but I'll scrape my knees on the ground while I give you the ride of your life!" I say. "You wouldn't want me to scrape my knees, would you?"

I grab his fat face with my right hand and press my lips roughly against his. All his protests, all his worries seem to melt away during that very first kiss.

His lips tremble. His gasps for air tickle my face. He's so excited, so overcome, I'm not sure he's going to last another second. His eyes shut and his shoulder slack.

I'm winning. Fuck it, I've got the jackpot already.

And then, he starts to give it some tongue and my insides turn even more mushy. I grab his head and kiss him more firmly. Deeply. Passionately.

I can't stop myself from moaning. From grinding into his big sexy body. I'm so wet. So horny. So desperate for him.

Never before have I had to wait this long before getting what I want. Most guys are pretty damn easy. But then they fizzle out and leave me wanting.

The anticipation drove him to the brink of insanity tonight, and now I realise, I wasn't far behind. I too have rubbed myself raw these past couple of weeks. I too have had too many orgasms to count, but none of them really hit the spot. Thinking about him. Imagining him sitting there in his flat, looking across at mine, watching everything I did. Everything I did for him.

"Baby, I need you. My body needs you," I whine.

We take a few steps back, still clinging together, but also desperate to make some progress towards the staircase.

"You're going to regret ever teasing me."

"Never."

"I'm going to destroy that sweet little pussy of yours!"

"I'm counting on it!"

I pull away and start walking faster. He stumbles behind me as fast as he can. Out of breath. Out of sorts. Around the various air vents and pipes and hoses. I have him by the arm, leading the way off the roof.

As soon as we make it into the staircase, he's on me again, pushing me against the rough concrete wall while wetly eating my face and grabbing my right breast for the first time.

That's almost enough to make me cum right there.

"Oh fuck!" I cry out. "Oh you know just how I like it!"

"I'm gonna tear that ass open!"

"It's yours. Do whatever you want with it!" This time he takes the lead and drags me down the stairs, one laboured step at a time. Sweat is dripping down his sideburns. His t-shirt is getting damp. Even his walk has changed, probably because his thick cock is getting in the way.

It makes me swell with pride to see him this desperately horny. He *has* been suffering like he said. As have I. If only he'd taken a moment to truly see me when we passed each other in the street, we could have been doing this all along. But then again, all this anticipation has made our upcoming encounter even hotter. I've always had a flair for the dramatic.

We burst through the door leading out of the staircase. He drags me roughly by my arm towards the elevators, where a confused bystander stumbles backwards out of our way.

Once the doors close behind us, he attacks again. His mouth, on the side of my neck, kissing, licking, nibbling all the way down to my collar bone.

I slip my hand underneath his t-shirt and grab a

handful of love handle, while at the same time grinding my knee up into his crotch.

"Fuck me," he growls. "You're a very bad girl, you know that?"

"You love it. You love every second of it. You'll love it even more when I sit on your cock later!"

He moans and closes his eyes while I pull myself closer into him. Rubbing my naked body all over his big round belly. God, he's sexy. Every inch and every pound. I need to feel his immense weight on top of me before the night is over. Maybe that'll finally scratch the itch I've been feeling for so long.

The elevator slows to signal our arrival on the correct floor. He pauses and looks at me for a moment. "Any moment now."

"Any moment, what?" I ask.

"Any moment now you'll change your mind."

I smile and shake my head while starting to peel his shirt up and off of him. He yanks it back down, panting for air. "No!"

"You don't want this?" I ask, while provocatively spreading my legs and reaching down and running my fingertip over the soaked material of my panties.

"Jesus fucking Christ."

"I'll make you feel good, baby. Let me make it all better for you!"

"Let's go to your place instead," he says.

I shrug. It'll be a longer walk. Maybe he's been so busy watching my flat through the windows that he wants to experience it first-hand now. A fantasy come true.

"Someone might see us," I warn.

He looks worried for a second, but his expression calms once I grin at him and lick my lips.

"You would like that, wouldn't you?" he asks.

My grin widens. "Someone might be on the other side of that door right now, in fact."

Him:

What the actual fuck just happened? I was out on the roof, cursing her for trapping me. Cursing myself for getting caught. I was so certain I'd fucked up worse than ever before. That my life was going to be over anyway once she sets the cops on me… Once they find all the evidence on my phone, on my pc. On the cloud, even. Hundreds upon hundreds of pictures of her, taken over the course of two short weeks.

All I wanted was for the pain to go away. Forever. I wasn't about to wait around and get arrested and have my freedom and dignity taken away from me too.

And she actually followed me. She saw what I was up to and had to intervene.

Who does that?

Who actually fucking runs after some loser up on the roof of an eighteen story building, while wearing nothing more than a few triangles of lace?

She does, apparently. This girl who's grinding up against me in the elevator. Kissing–no, devouring me. And I don't even know her name.

Except for how fucking gorgeous she looks naked, I know nothing about her.

Okay, well, I know what she smells like now. Sweet and flowery and fresh. And what her lips taste like. I know how soft her skin feels underneath my touch. Despite the goose bumps, because she's still freezing after being out there half-naked.

I know the silkiness of her hair. Exactly how it looked on maximum zoom on my phone.

This really isn't supposed to happen. Not to me. I'm not supposed to be here.

She's not supposed to touch me. Any moment now someone else will find us and it'll all end.

My heart starts to race even more than it already had. Maybe the cops are waiting for us at her flat right now. Maybe this is all a ploy to get me caught.

The elevator doors open, but the hallway outside is eerily quiet. No movement. No sound of police radios. Nothing.

I'm frozen in place, stunned. Until her hand grabs mine, tugging on it until I walk out of the confined space, behind her.

God, that ass.

That tight little ass, sashaying from side to side as she walks. She's doing it on purpose, just like everything else she's done so far. Nobody has a natural walk like that.

And the worst part is, it works. It fucking works so well on me. I can't look away.

She turns her head once we reach her front door. She smiles that same little smile at me which I've seen on her before. That same smile I interpreted as a taunt every single time I saw it.

She's laughing at you. She's laughing because she knows you can't back up all the filthy shit you said to her earlier. The fucking whore.

"Baby, close the door behind you," she tells me. Her voice is sugary sweet. It's fake; has to be. Nobody has ever spoken to me like this.

Except maybe that one time I called a sex line. Girls will only speak to me like this if they're getting paid.

What's the catch with her? When will she demand her compensation? Or when will the cops turn up. Maybe she does have a boyfriend and he's on the way over to beat the shit out of me. Maybe that's what's getting her off. She's already anticipating my complete humiliation.

"The bedroom's through here. But you already know that." She licks both her lips, before biting down on the bottom one.

Fuck. What even am I doing right now?

I shake my head. I can't go in there. I can't do this. It's a trap. It's all a trap.

"What's wrong?" she asks.

As if she doesn't know.

I keep on shaking my head, but the words just don't come.

The curtains are still open. The windows, too. I feel so exposed in here, with the whole world watching my inevitable downfall from across the building.

Holy shit, how did she do this every night? How did

she make a display of herself, knowing that absolutely everyone in the other side of the building can see.

She claims she did it for me, but that doesn't make any sense.

Why am I here?

"I don't belong here," I mumble. "This isn't my scene."

"Sweetheart, you're the only one I want in here with me."

"Stop lying!" I snap.

She flinches, but then takes a couple of steps back in my direction. I still can't believe how flawless she looks in that outfit. Like a model. Or a mannequin.

"What do I have to do to convince you?" she asks. Gone is the sweetness and playfulness in her tone. This is transactional now.

"You can't. Because this is wrong."

No matter how much my cock throbs and aches in my boxers. No matter how bittersweet the ache in my chest, roughly where my heart is. I can't do this. I can't give her what she wants.

She sits on the edge of the bed and leans back on her elbows.

"At least sit with me. Talk it out."

I shake my head, but there's something in her pleading eyes which forces my legs into action, seemingly against my will. One foot in front of the other, until I'm right next to her, lowering myself onto the bed. It looks solid enough, but fuck I hope it holds.

She places her hand on my thigh, palm facing

upwards.

So inviting, I can't help but grab it. My heart stops for a moment. The room stops spinning out of control.

"I'm sorry I teased you so mercilessly every night," she says.

I glance over at her. She really does look remorseful. What an actress.

"I shouldn't have been looking."

She cocks her head to the side. "I get it, okay? You're feeling guilty about what happened. But you did nothing wrong. I was at fault, right from the start."

I shake my head again. No.

"No, I'm serious," she says. "I hurt you. I didn't mean to, but that doesn't make it any better."

I take a deep breath, but don't quite know what to say, so I keep quiet.

"Give me the chance to make it better. I'll do whatever you need."

Fuck. What I need is to make good on my words from earlier, and tear that sweet little pussy of hers up. I need to bury my cock in her so deeply, she can feel it tickle when I shoot my load.

One of many. Because once isn't going to be enough.

I'm going to have to do that over and over and over again. Fuck her out of my system. Get my sanity back over blood, sweat and cum.

"I…"

"I know we don't know each other. But I meant everything, okay? I would miss you, if you weren't there." She nods at the window, or rather, at my window which is visible from her window. "If you weren't there in your flat. I do care."

No, she doesn't. Nobody does. She can't help me.

I need to go take care of the searing ache in my crotch. And this bullshit conversation isn't going to do it. I try to shift my weight a little. Just enough to stop my belly from weighing down on my cock so hard. Fuck, if I keep doing that, I might just blow my load right now.

"Baby, you're hurting. I can see it," she says. Her voice has changed again. It's more raw than before. Breathier.

The sound drives me crazy all over again.

"I am," I whisper under my breath. Fuck, I'm hurting so much. Not just physically.

"Let me help you then." She gets up off the bed, walks over to the window and shuts the curtains. I don't know what to say. Along with the last remnants of daylight, there goes my voice.

"No," I whimper.

She shakes her head. "Baby, trust me. We both need this."

"No! I'm not worthy!" I cry out. My chest is on fire. I can't breathe. Every time I close my eyes, I see fragmented images of her, straddled on top of me. Tits swinging freely as she rides me.

"Shut up, you gorgeous man. Let me make it better."

I press my lips together and watch her as she unclasps her bra from behind, and lets it fall. Not the first time I've seen her tits, but the first time up close.

It's different when it's not fuzzy because of camera zoom.

She gets down on her knees in front of me, and starts tugging at my sweatpants. They're going nowhere while I'm sitting down. I really shouldn't– I should keep sitting–

I lift my hips to help her peel them off of me. Not sure why I do that. The sneaky girl takes my boxers down with them before I get the chance to stop her.

Here I am. Buck naked. On this beautifully made bed. Clean sheets which smell of jasmine flowers. That's what that scent is, which I noticed clinging to her hair…

She crawls closer, and runs her hand up my thigh. Up, up, up, to where my belly touches, and gets it into the deep fold there, until she finds my cock.

Her cold hand soothes me and heats me up all at once. Fuck, it burns. I could come in five seconds flat at this rate.

I must have made a sound to that effect, because she pulls away again.

"Baby, lie back for me," she whispers.

I don't want to. And at the same time, it's all I want.

She gets up, giving me an eyeful of bare nipple. They're hard. She must still be cold. Yet she warms my lips with hot breaths when she leans down before kissing me again.

My vision goes black. I let myself fall backwards, helpless to her charms. This is a beautiful fantasy. Unreal. Too good to be true.

"I can't," I mumble. It's hard to speak with your mouth full of tongue. Impossible to concentrate when you've got your hands full of plump breasts. And an angel, straddling your thighs will wipe your mind free of conflicting thoughts.

"Shift up a little," she instructs.

It's a nearly impossible task while I'm on my back like this, but I try anyway.

She shuffles down, then grabs my belly, shifting it up just enough, and then…

Heaven. Sweet sticky heat envelops my cock. All the way from the tip to the end of the shaft. She's done it. Or rather, she's undone me.

I can't move. Can't breathe. I'm one vibration away from cumming.

She didn't even put a condom on me. There wasn't time.

I must be dreaming.

But when I look up, I see the truth in her eyes. This isn't a dream. It's so much better.

My cock is pulsating with anticipation, yet she doesn't move either. She just sits there, on top of me, with a content half-smile on her face. Like she's won the lottery.

I've won the lottery.

Holy shit, what do I even say now?

"Baby," she murmurs. "I want you to cum for me."

As she says that, her pussy squeezes down hard on my cock, and I'm lost. Gone. Dead.

My balls tighten in waves, forcing hot cum up

through my shaft and into her. I can actually feel it. Normally I'm never this aware. But now…

I can feel it gushing, spurting, filling her up.

She moans deeply, squeezing down on me again, and grinding against my fat belly ever so subtly. I'm frozen in place. She almost has to pry my fingers open when she lifts my hand onto her ass.

For once in my life, I know what to do. I weigh her down into me, pulling her into the soft fleshy pad surrounding my cock, making it so I'm even deeper inside of her. And then I help her grind against it some more. Back and forth, ever so slightly, but never loosening my grip on her.

All the while I'm still depositing my cum in her vagina. Holy shit, I didn't know I had that much to give.

I look up and see tears in her wide eyes as she loudly cries out. "Fuck me!"

Oh sweetheart, if only I could. The best I can do for her is to keep her moving, while she shudders and trembles and moans and whimpers.

Before collapsing in a heap on top of me and tearing at my t-shirt with her fingernails.

"Oh my God!" she moans.

I concur, but I haven't caught my breath yet. She did cum too, right? I mean… What else was all the drama for?

But I don't get the chance to ask her, or do much of anything else, because she's sitting up on me again, and this time she's moving a lot more. Up and down in longer, more controlled strokes, with her hand finding leverage on my very substantial love handles.

And despite cumming in record time, I'm still rock hard. That's the effect she's been having on me all along. Even from a distance. One orgasm never does the trick.

"You're so hot," she gasps.

I don't believe her. But, as long as she keeps going, does it really matter?

"Fuck, you're perfect," she whines. One hand reaches up towards the centre of my chest and grabs my t-shirt, hard. Then, with a firm pull, the fabric starts to tear right down the middle. I don't know whether to be shocked or impressed. Probably a bit of both.

She squeals when she slips her hand inside, petting my hairy chest for the very first time.

Earlier I'd stopped her from taking my shirt off. Now, I can't. It's anyway too late.

Or... it feels so very good that I don't want to anymore. No, *I* feel so very good, better than I ever have before, that I don't have the will to intervene.

She carries on petting me with one hand, while riding me on her bed.

Holy shit I'm in this girl's flat. In her bed. And she's having her way with me. This was all *her* idea. All of it. I said I didn't want to.

Of course I wanted nothing more, but I couldn't admit it, even to myself. Thank god she didn't listen to me.

Just like that, I feel another wave build. No, this time I need to draw it out. I can't keep cumming within seconds every time. That's pathetic.

"Oh baby, I love your hairy chest!" she moans. "You're so sexy!"

I close my eyes and try to regain my composure. She's riding me faster now. Her tight little ass is bobbing up and down on me at a relentless pace. Her pussy is so tight, it's still gripping me firmly. But it's also so wet. So very slippery. That helps a little in warding off the inevitable.

She leans down and nuzzles my chest. Jesus Christ. I never knew I needed to be touched there. And then, she takes my nipple into her mouth and my mind goes blank with sensations I'd never even imagined before.

I can't stop it. I can't keep quiet. I can't…

My cock erupts again and this time I'm the one who screams senseless expletives.

But instead of stopping to make fun of me, she runs the tip of her tongue across my nipple and kills me even further.

In my dazed state, I figure maybe she's sending a message. Maybe she wants the same thing too. I can't reach her with my mouth like this, so instead I grab hold of her right tit and run my thumb across the hard centre. Circling, circling, flicking across it ever so lightly, just like she's doing with her mouth. That's her cue to speed up. Harder and faster she rides me. She's so quick, I'm not sure I've ever seen anything like it even in porn.

The room is quiet, except for the incessant sound of flesh slapping against flesh. And feverish breaths, failing to keep up with the rhythm she's set. The musky scent of sex hangs in the air.

Until suddenly, she stops. I wrap my arms around her athletic little body, cradling her on top of me, as she trembles uncontrollably all over. Not just her back, her arms, her thighs, but even her cunt. As if she's trying to draw the final drops of cum out of me. Again.

It doesn't even occur to me to think about whether she'd want to cuddle with me. It just feels natural to hold her while she's quivering on top of me. I soothe her and listen to her breaths calm along with mine. I caress her hair and kiss the side of her head as it rests against my chin.

I close my eyes and smile when her fingers dig into my shoulder as if to say: "Don't let me go."

It's a moment of bliss, the likes of which I've never experienced before.

"Baby, you're the best," she whispers. Or maybe I just imagine that, because it's what I really, really want to hear.

And as soon as she finishes her sentence, I can feel a familiar feeling grow in me. A familiar urge. One I've tried to stamp out for two weeks now, to no avail.

My cock, still buried inside her, grows a little thicker again. Just a little harder…

Her hips stir. She can feel it.

My filthy angel lifts her head and looks down on me with that same Mona Lisa smile.

"You can go again?" she asks.

I shrug, sheepishly, even though she looks impressed

rather than disheartened.

"With you, I could go all night," I say.

She lets out a little gasp, then grins widely. "Finally a guy who can keep up with my appetite. I knew there was something special about you from the moment I saw you."

I don't know what to say to that, so I just smile back at her. Maybe all the time I thought I'd wasted building up stamina with my right hand was well spent after all. Just maybe, the thing I thought made me useless and a waste of space, is exactly what she needs to feel satisfied. Sounds like she never had that before. What a fucking shame. This girl deserves all the pleasure in the world.

I just can't get over one thing yet.

"You don't care that I'm… you know. This big?" I ask.

This time her smile isn't subtle anymore. It's bright as the midday sun.

"Are you kidding? Every inch of you is perfect. Regular sized guys can't even get me moist and ever since I first saw you two weeks ago, I've been gushing all day!"

Fuck, she has a filthy mouth and I love it.

She leans down and kisses me hard, like only she can do. I grab the back of her neck and give it right back to her until she whimpers into my mouth. I thought she was acting earlier. What a fucking idiot I was. I thought she was faking it to trap me. Finally, I can see the truth. This horny little angel was being totally honest with me.

She did leave her curtains open for me to see her nightly shows. She did finger herself raw, simply for me to watch her do it. And now she has been giving me the ride of my life just now, because it pleases her just as much.

I grab her ass cheek with my other hand, marvelling at just how good it feels to be growing to my maximum length and girth inside of her again. Until she pulls away from our frantic make-out session.

"No way. This time, I wanna be on my back!" she demands.

I press my lips together. How will that even work?

"Won't I be too heavy for you?"

Her:

His question makes me smile again. Just because I'm smaller doesn't make me fragile. And our size difference is the whole point why I want it. It's just no fun for me having a skinny guy between my thighs. I should have realized that years ago instead of chasing the wrong men.

I shake my head.

"It's going to be awesome, trust me," I tell him.

He watches helplessly as I get off him and lay further up the bed on my back. He turns onto his side first, then struggles breathlessly to get onto all fours next to me. This is obviously not a position he's used to.

I wonder if he was a virgin before today. Not because his technique lacks anything, but simply because he was being so weird with me earlier. Probably would be wiser not to ask, in case the question freaks him out all over again.

The partly torn t-shirt hangs off his chest, giving me an eyeful of furry man-cleavage. Further down, it's still intact and clings to his big belly as it sags down heavily beneath him. He really is a large man. Supersized, you could say. It's a sight to behold.

I spread as far as I can and wait for him to get into position.

His eyes are a bit wide again. Fearful for what's to come. But when I reach down past his big fat belly, I can just about feel his thick cock, ready for action. I knew he wouldn't let me down.

If he wasn't a virgin, then certainly this is the first time he's ever been on top, I decide. The thought that this might be a first for him is making me even more horny. It's a first for me too. My first time with a supersized guy. My first time being filled up with cum twice in such quick succession. He did say up to ten times. We're going to test those limits, though maybe not until we get a good night's sleep and a proper meal. Because now that I have him, I'm never letting go.

He's hesitating. Fumbling. Trying to get into position between my thighs while losing his breath. It would be adorable, if I wasn't also so desperate for his cock.

"Here," I tell him, while lifting my hips up in his direction. "Lift up your belly and slip it in."

His eyes meet mine for a brief moment. He looks uncomfortable. Like I'm asking for the world.

It reminds of the look on his face up on the roof earlier. His guilt for watching me nearly killed me. And then once we got here, how hard he fought to prevent any of this from happening. Though I could see so clearly he needed it. We both did.

I put my hand on the side of his face and keep looking at him. Whispering sweet encouragements to him.

"Trust me. This'll be amazing."

His brow is sweaty already. Laboured breaths hit my face and chest. This is going to be hard on him, physically. But with a little help from my right hand, and some minor contortionist moves to get myself lined up with my legs straight up, the tip of his dick finds my entrance and we're finally good to go.

"Come down," I whisper, resting my hand flat on his big fleshy shoulder. I wish he wasn't still wearing that torn t-shirt, but considering how weird he's been all through, I didn't dare ask him to take it off.

Next time, I decide.

He lets out an involuntary groan as he gets down onto his elbows on top of me. I'm trapped in the soft mattress. Weighed down by his humongous torso. Soft, pliable flesh envelops me, making it harder to breathe.

But it's also so good, though.

I try to wiggle my ass a little, get his cock to slip in deeper. It's nearly impossible until he shifts his hips just so, and it slides in all the way.

"Ohhh!" I cry out.

He rests his forehead against mine. His eyes close.

He's still panting quite fast, even if he isn't moving much at all.

My baby needs a bit of practice, which is fine. This is all new to him, after all.

I, meanwhile, am in heaven. Running my hands up his big arms. So squishy. So perfect.

His shoulders, which are at least twice as broad as mine. I caress his sides, fondling and squishing any roll and lump of flesh within reach. I scratch my fingernails across his back and grab his ass. Hard.

That's all he needed to get moving. Slowly but surely, he starts to rut into me. It must take a lot to get all this mass in motion. He's still sweating. Still squeezing his eyes shut in concentration.

"Hell yeah! So good!" I moan.

Every time he thrusts into me, even this slowly and gently, he knocks the wind out of my lungs. I have no choice but to adjust my breaths to his rhythm.

He tries to change it up, find the right motion, the right speed. All his muscles are working hard to keep up with this new activity. I can tell, by the funny tremble that creeps across his hips and back and shoulders every so often.

And the loud groans escaping his lips when he struggles for air.

But his dick feels as glorious as it did with me on top. Even better, in fact.

How he stretches me out to accommodate him. The burn in my hips makes the experience all the more delicious.

And the stabbing pain in my chest that I get every time I try to breathe with his weight on me. Holy fuck. It takes things to a whole new level.

He's the sexiest man alive. And he's all mine right now. Couldn't move away even if he wanted to for as long as I cling to him.

He fucks me slowly. Fighting gravity with every stroke. The tense scowl on his face tells me this is the hardest he's ever had to fight.

I love it.

I love how he's giving himself to me.

I love him for it.

Hell, I think I started to fall from the moment he confessed his darkest thoughts. From the moment I saw his fears and vulnerabilities. How he kept repeating he can't do this and he's not supposed to be here. He's carrying so much guilt. So much self-hate. Like he's blaming himself for lusting after me.

Does he not realize that's what he's supposed to do, as a man? It's simple biology. He's supposed to want to empty his balls in me. What else are they there for? And I've been asking for it from the moment I started leaving my curtains open for him.

No, what we're doing right now isn't wrong at all. Everything is happening exactly as it's meant to. I am his and he is mine. We are fulfilling our destiny with every stroke.

And he's still fucking me. Slowly. Deliberately. Thrusting into me with his full weight, then pulling out just enough to soothe the ache in the base of my clit with his shaft. Hey moves like a huge wave, first crashing then withdrawing. Every movement amplified in his fat body. Flesh rippling along, helping as well as hampering his progress all at once.

What an experience. What a treat.

"Does that feel good?" I ask him.

It's obvious that it does. His expression is calmer now, almost serene, ever since he found his rhythm. But I still want to hear it.

"You…Have…No…Idea," he pants.

The fact that he can hardly speak makes me even hotter. Though this is far from the pace I'm accustomed to, I can feel a familiar tightness build in my lower abdomen. It's nice, actually. At this pace, I can feel every little sensation leading up to my release in so much detail.

I feel connected to him. And I need to show him that I do.

So, I let go of his back and grab his face, guiding it down into me until our lips meet again.

His eyes open. His gorgeous blue eyes. I never noticed just how sparkly blue they were until I got into bed with him.

He sighs and pauses, with his cock buried as far inside of me as it'll go. And almost his full weight on me. We stare at each other, while my tongue seeks out his lips. Gentle licks and kisses, to tell him how much I appreciate what he's doing for me. How much I appreciate *him*.

He moans into my mouth. It's real and raw and

vulnerable. The most beautiful noise I ever heard.

"Baby I'm going to need this every night," I whisper.

His eyes widen, before flagging slightly when I contract my cunt. Every night. Every day. I'm going to train him up like my personal sex slave, until this movement becomes natural to him. Until his stamina outlasts my own.

"Never gonna let you go."

He tenses all over, and starts to move again. His hips speed up just a bit faster than before. He's getting the hang of this. My pussy is still aching, but every movement of his manages to calm me just a little.

And on top of that, all the other sensations I feel in my body are amplified a thousand fold. There's a tickle in my chest I never felt before. Like butterflies, only sweeter. A tingling sensation in my arms and hands, urging me to touch him all over, just to feel the warmth in his skin again.

A breathlessness that is only soothed the more I kiss him. Slowly, to match his love-making.

I realize now that that's what it is.

I *fucked* him earlier. Because that's what we needed to get out of the way. But now he's making love to me. And it's beautiful. Perfect. It's everything I need without me ever asking for it.

A droplet of sweat rolls down his nose, dripping down onto my cheek. It tickles, making me giggle. I grin into his lips and tighten my arms around his neck. It's the only place I can comfortably hug on him. The rest of his torso is just too large for me to reach around properly.

I don't know him. Not really. Beyond the fears he confessed to me and the noises he makes when he's close to cumming. I know hardly anything about him. But I feel more intimately connected to him than I could have ever imagined. I don't even know his name, yet I know he's the one I want. The only one I'll ever need.

He's the one man who could satisfy me. With his thick cock and even thicker body, his supply of cum seemingly as limitless as his waistline…

I grab his big man tit, weighing it in my hand as he carries on grinding into me. He seemed to love it when I sucked on it earlier. In this position, he'll have to make do with just my fingers. Squeezing, kneading, tweaking his nipples like most of the men I've been with have liked to do to me. I figure they do it because that's what they want. They want it rougher.

He's no exception. The way he squirms under my touch. Speeding up. Groans growing ever louder.

What started off as a tightness and a tickle in my uterus is turning into a powerful swell of sweet pain. I'm right there with him, on the precipice. Holding to unleash the tension as soon as he is.

We've been going for a while now. Slowly. Steadily. Moving in unison, breathing in tandem. But now, with both my hands on his tits, thumbing his nipples over and over again, he's sprinting to the finish line. At his own pace, of course.

I don't mind this time. Or any time before. I don't

care that he came so quickly the last two times. Because it didn't stop the action. Neither did my own orgasms. We were ready to go again within seconds.

Nothing unusual for me, but such staying power is a very pleasant surprise to find in a man.

What is unusual now, is that I *feel so* different. The build-up for this release is unlike all the others. It has more gravitas. More meaning.

I feel it more deeply, like it affects not just my cunt but my entire being.

Looking at his face, scrunched up in concentration, I wonder if it's the same for him. Will this orgasm actually satisfy? Will its aftereffects last?

He bucks into me, giving it a little bit of upward motion. It's new. I love it.

And although I'd been trying to hold off the inevitable, the floodgates blast open for me.

I scream. So much tension. So much pain. All released at once.

My body contorts and trembles underneath him. I try to clamp down on his cock to force him over the edge too, but my pussy is no longer under my control.

I wish I knew his name so I could serenade him with it. Let him know that it's him—and only him—I credit for this. An orgasm like no other.

He might not have done it like he said he would; by pounding my pussy into submission, but he's achieved it nonetheless. I've been defeated. I'm dying for him, just a little bit.

And right in the middle of it, he stops.

Frozen, with his eyes wide shut, he's weighing me down. My lungs empty for the most part. They've got no choice, weighed down as they are. My pussy is still on fire. My chest is bursting with sensations I've never felt before. Tears sting in my eyes.

At last, my vision goes dark.

He's stuck on top of me, seemingly holding his breath. Time stands still, until I feel it.

His cock, quivering deep inside. As deep as it could go, given the constraints of his big body. Tickling me right at the g-spot as he unloads. For the third time this hour and still completely unlike the other two times.

This is it. The one. The one orgasm to rule them all.

As I threaten to black out, I realize just what this means. After a build-up that has lasted for two weeks now. We've made it. We've finally scratched the itch.

I caress his face. It's different from before. Calmer. At peace.

Not sure how much time passes before he stirs again, rolling off to the side, allowing me to finally fill my lungs completely again.

I gasp for air, lightheaded and overcome.

His arms find me, tugging me close to him. His hand caresses my hair, my shoulder.

I don't even remember anymore what I expected, knowing him only from afar. But I never expected this depth of affection or sensitivity.

With his thick beard and guarded eyes, I thought maybe he would just smash and leave. Emotionless and without substance, like all the others.

I never missed anyone once they left.

With him… everything is different. I ache for that next touch. That next caress. I could die for another kiss.

He's still catching his breath when I drape my thigh across his and wrap my arm around him as far as it'll go. Resting my temple against his shoulder, I know. This is it now. I've found the man for me. Someone to share my body with, maybe even my soul. Both are his for as long as he wants me.

Definitely never letting him go if it's up to me.

And I don't even know his name.

ABOUT THE AUTHOR

Dear Reader,

If you came across me in real life, you'd never guess the kind of filth I like to read and write. Cleverly disguised as a boring office worker, the drudgery of my 9-to-5 only because bearable because of my vivid and explicit imagination. I like fat guys and I cannot lie. In my world, bigger (fatter) is always better. It's been that way for as long as I can remember.

Thanks for reading this story, one of hopefully many of my published sexual fantasies. My stories revolve around one common theme: really big men and the women who can't help but lust for them.

Although I like porn just fine, it's nearly impossible to find it in the flavour that I desire. The written word allows me to explore a world of lush excess that mainstream adult entertainment just cannot provide. When I started writing, I soon discovered the beauty of having a catalog of erotica out there to satisfy my own lustful needs. This is a passion project more than a money-grab.

So, first and foremost, my writing is for me. But perhaps there are other women (or even men) out there who share my tastes; my fetishes and fantasies? My fascination with the larger male form, and sexualisation of food (especially overeating). If that sounds like something you'll wank off to, you've come to the right place.

xxx Hedonist

To find out more, check:

❖   eXplicitTales.com